AMBROSIA NIGHTS

By Kristy Nicolle

Queens Of Fantasy Saga
An Aetherial Embrace Short Story

First published by Kristy Nicolle, United Kingdom, October 2019

QUEENS OF FANTASY EDITION (1st EDITION)

Published October 2019 by: Kristy Nicolle

Edited by: Jaimie Cordall

Adult Paranormal/Fantasy Romance

Disclaimer:

This ebook is written in U.K English by personal preference of the author. This is a work of fiction. Names, characters, businesses, places, events and incidents are either the products of the author's imagination or used in a fictitious manner. Any resemblance to actual persons, living or dead, or actual events is purely coincidental.

ISBN: 978-1-911395-20-1

www.kristynicolle.com

For all the storytellers who came before.

Ambrosia Nights

APOLLO

"Aphrodite, are you coming?" My voice reverberates around the spacious lobby of our home with its pristine high ceilings and flawless milky floors.

"God, Pol. Give a girl a second!" she calls back from upstairs as she suddenly appears at the top of the minimalist floating staircase.

"If you call me Pol one more time, then I'm going to have to resort to calling you Aphro—" I threaten, completely at ease with my body as I take in her descending form with an objective eye. Her reflective golden hair is pulled up into a relaxed bun on the crown of her head, several white gold strands falling around her face and making her beauty delicate.

Her gown is floor length, slimming her form. It shimmers like a rose gold star as it hits the pure light of the platinum twilight pouring generously through the wide surrounding windows.

I run my fingers through my multicoloured hair, clad in a loose-fitting white shirt and black leggings. My thick soled

1

leather boots are loud against the floor, meshing in an oxy-moronic yet gendered melody as Aphrodite's heels touch down against the slick white marble. She holds out a hand to me, which I take. Her skin is like silk upon my calloused artist's palm.

"Any particular reason for this little night on the town?" she demands with the sensuous purr she knows all too well I'm immune to. A shawl woven heavy with thousands of miniscule diamonds is slung over her arms, and it almost blinds me as she turns to tilt her head. Her face is expectant, presenting me with a familiar shimmering pout.

"You've seemed — I don't know — sad lately. I thought seeing as Hermes has a new batch of Ambrosia coming in that we might as well seize the opportunity," I explain, ap-praising her stunning face, but finding no arousal, no lust for her. I love this woman, far more than I've ever loved anyone, but it is nothing to do with the sexual energy that pours off her like thick, sweet honey. I have never found, nor will ever find, sexual desire toward another, even her.

No, instead, my appreciation is purely artistic; of the way her lips curve just so, of how her eyes are shaped just provocatively enough to lure interest from the most unsus-pecting of hearts, the visual equivalent of a siren's lure. She's a masterpiece of divine design, there is no doubt, but beyond that, her soul is the most beautiful thing I've ever seen. Our home is scattered with what I consider to be poor representations of that face, of what lies beneath the gossamer veil of her flesh, but that which she claims is some of my best work.

"Your chariot awaits, m'lady." I give a mock bow and she giggles, gazing with hooded lids back over one bare shoulder as she strides past me. As her best friend, I know her tricks, but I also know her freedom in wielding them is what's causing her such pain.

The revolving glass door marks the entrance to our gallery-esque place of residence, sitting central to the Artist's quarter on the outermost edge of Olympolis. As ever, I'm thankful our journey into the city will be short. Following Aphrodite's sparkling silhouette, her permanent scent of violets, roses, and sweet vanilla cream is unchanging as it causes my heartbeat to slow where others might quicken.

Out on the golden cobblestones, they stand, Pyrois, Aeos, Aethon, and Phlegon. Their bodies are slick with short golden coats that gleam as though they've been doused in oil. Their manes crackle and blaze into the evening air, tongues of flame casting the golden stones of the surrounding floor aflame in a stark contrast to the pastel lemon of the twilight overhead. Eyes blazing with a passion that cannot be contained, their nostrils flare, blood racing around their tight, muscular bodies, desperate to run long, hard, and free.

Striding over to them, my nose empties of Aphrodite and fills instead with the fresh scent of buttercups and early morning dew, the aroma of their buttery breaths mingling with the soap stable-hands have used to groom them.

White gold chains link them to my pride and joy, the mere sight of it causing me to beam. It is ostentatious perhaps, but seeing as I'm the God of all things aesthetic, I had thought, why not?

Aphrodite catches me gawping at it and rolls her eyes, taking the sheath of her glittering skirt between two slender fingers and carefully stepping up into the hold of the *Solar-Flare* model chariot. It is one of only three in existence and the only one in Olympus. Unrivalled in speed or distinctiveness, its gilded body and wheels cast a gentle spray of golden sparks in its wake for no other reason than that the Titan who had sold it to me has a thing for glamour enchantments.

Aphrodite begins to look impatient, as she often does with me, as I dawdle in the gilded circular courtyard. My mind is rarely cohesive, more often scattered between this world and somewhere else entirely, too occupied with words, brush strokes, and sculpting some daydream into reality to find the real world much of a fascination.

I close the distance between myself and the vehicle at her increasing silent insistence, passing the barely noticed fountain that tinkles on my left.

After hoisting myself up into the hold of the chariot, my fingers caressing the golden curves of the frame in wordless appreciation, Aphrodite passes me the reins with a sigh.

"You know, you could always let me drive." She pouts. I roll my eyes.

Chuckling, her metallic silver irises tinge ever so slightly pink in her amused exasperation beneath the dying gold weep of the skies.

"Nobody drives the *Solar Flare* except me. You know how these horses are—" I protest, but she simply rolls her eyes again, sculpted mouth turning up into a beautifully measured smile. It is no wonder to me as I stare at her that this same smile has shattered hearts long thought made of stone.

"So you keep telling everyone. I just think you're worried I'll show you up." She baits me, cyelashes tremoring like the wings of a butterfly. For any other man, this small action alone would bring him to his knees, but not I. Perhaps that's why, after all these years, Aphrodite and I remain so close.

"You've seen them run at the Panathenaic Stadium; do you really want to try driving them?" I open my palms, letting the glowing reins lie flat, and watch as her eyes widen and then narrow, suspicious.

"You would let a lady drive herself?" She gives a coy smile, brushing a white gold strand from her forehead with a gentle stroke of her index finger. I smile.

"I thought not." Smirking to myself, I let my fists curl around the reins and give a sharp yank, watching the flaming manes of the stallions grow longer as they start into wild forward motion.

Aphrodite sits on the plush leather bench I had fitted, fingers wrapping around the grab rail that's nailed into the upholstery, unmoving and graceful as she peers out into the world beyond the golden rim. We leave the artist's quarter with its fountains that bleed paint of every hue and the pavements which, when viewed from an aerial perspective, become masterpieces in their own glimmering right.

The Plati-sun continues to fall ever closer to the mountainous silhouette of the horizon until finally meeting with the skyline of Vulcan, City of Forges. The glistening sphere of light best known for its purity is lost behind the endless billow of smoke and soot, and for only the briefest of moments, the Higher Plains is plunged into almost complete darkness. I stare up into the sky's inky spill, the only light being long dead celestial souls overhead, swirling within galaxies inside universes.

Moments pass, but the world is not left unattended for long as on the opposite side of the landscape, a prismic crystal moon peeks just over the edge, sleepily opening one lunar eye and yawning as its borrowed light throws everything into the underappreciated glory of nightfall.

I glimpse down at Aphrodite as she lets one elbow drape over the rim of the chariot, her silver irises reflecting the sky within their mercurial depths.

I tear my gaze away from her, knowing I need to focus on steering the horses that have been transformed by the contrast of the surrounding night into stallion-shaped earth-bound suns, but I find her unassuming admiration of the natural world beautiful in itself.

Our journey continues in haste, and all is silent except for the clipping of flaming hooves against the golden cobbles forming one of the many brightly hued and spidering transport veins into the city. The scent of Olympolis central slowly drifts in on a cool twilight mist that descends suddenly as we near in our approach. Our steeds illuminate the cool vapour the colour of burning coals, and the contrast with the white marble of towering skyscrapers, decorated with what seems to be infinite skyward pillars in milky white, is magical. The scent of honey, myrrh, and sweet olives intoxicates me as I let go of the events of the day, abandoning thoughts of the odd meeting with Haedes and his claims of otherworldly shift as my shoulders sag and my grip on the reins loosens.

The horses know their way around this city better than even I can claim, and so I take a moment to stare at the silver sidewalks. Illuminated by glass orbs filled with lone light-ning bolts as they fly by, the skyline of the city rises around the blazing golden comet, bringing us closer to its vibrant heart.

Minutes pass, the rhythmic trot of the steeds offering a familiar comfort. Finally, we take a left and enter the major artery of the city's most bustling district.

An enormous golden statue of Zeus atop a solid platinum throne rising from a reflecting pool meets us, the epicentre of the urban sprawl. Aquamarine waters remain stone-still around the King of The Gods, the tranquil pool a flawless mirror for the heavens over which he rules made material so they might ripple and quake at his feet.

Zeus' cold gaze seems to track the chariot as it rounds the edge of the pool, sparks flying out noticeably in the glass windows of surrounding spas, bath houses, dance halls, tai-lors, dress-makers, and cobblers. The sparks are not the only thing pulling attention though, as people out for the evening start running in our wake, waving and shouting.

By the time the horses draw to a halt outside the ambrosia bar, there is a crowd of bodies surrounding both us and the vehicle.

"Hey, out of the way!" I hear a familiar male voice boom, and the crowd of Titan bodies draped in fine silks and velvets turn as one to face our rescuer.

"Ares," I mutter under my breath.

The enormous body of Zeus' favourite son blankets the crowd in shadow as he steps off the glistening silver sidewalk and into the street.

His dark hair and beard are cast spectacular with metallic sheen as he's illuminated by one of the many crackling bottled lightning bolts strung overhead. His armour, the point of which at this hour and place evading me entirely, is turned further brassy, as though it's recently been drenched in blood for aesthetic purposes only. He holds out a hand, which I know isn't for me, and Aphrodite silently takes it as he pulls her out of the mass of adoring bystanders.

I, however, am not offered aid.

Asshole, I think as I push myself through the throng of grabby hands and hungry eyes after them.

I find them both under the silver silk awning of the venue, which is propped up by more Grecian pillars, the telltale architecture of the city and its divine origins.

I give a passing nod to the valet, who stands behind a solid sapphire pillar. "Careful with the horses, they're volatile — but you already know that." I warn the young male Titan, who is dressed in a simple silver toga, pinned at one shoulder with the golden crest of Hermes, who still can't let go of the retro attire fad of three years ago. I glimpse back over one shoulder, eyeing the crowd as the stallions whinny and then gallop away, a comet trail of sparks the only sign that they were ever there. As the vehicle departs, the crowd swells, and I watch outstretched hands drawing nearer as Titans try to lay claim to my skin.

What are they looking for?

Perhaps inspiration for some half-baked sketch or a beast wilting in untended clay, the strength to string words together in a way so divine they break the heart and fracture the soul of any who beholds them. Or maybe they just want to say they've met a celebrity. One of the more powerful gods.

People, particularly Titans who were once Kindred, and before even that Humans, are the strangest, most fragile, and yet the most resilient creatures.

"Thanks for that." I roll my eyes as I eventually turn to face Ares, running my fingers through my windswept rainbow locks. Ensuring the sarcastic expression has passed before I am fully facing him, I cross my arms defensively.

"My pleasure, dearest Apollo," Ares retorts, but his eyes aren't on me. They're raking across Aphrodite's exposed skin instead. I step behind the divide of gold-leaf strung into a thick cord and onto the cobalt velvet runner spilling from the front doors of the venue, observing her closely for a signal. Aphrodite looks uncomfortable, turning to face me, but he brings her hand quickly to his lips before she can pull away despite her obvious distaste.

Like father, like son — I think to myself, looping my arm through Aphrodite's and carrying out our well-practiced evasive manoeuvres.

I look up into his torn expression, his broad shadow darkening the rainbow of my hair and casting usually imperceptible lines of my face into shadow. I could invite him inside with us, but to be honest, I would rather gargle Zeus' hot urine.

He takes the hint, stepping aside and nodding to us both.

"Have a lovely evening. I should get home to Artemis." Neither of us disagrees with that sentiment, and yet he still has to physically drag his gaze from Aphrodite's placid quicksilver stare before he stalks off down the sidewalk, his tread leaving a slight rumble in its wake.

"You all right?" I enquire as she exhales breath and slumps, her façade of perfection slipping for but a second. She glances back over her shoulder to the crowd of eager eyes beyond the gold-leaf divide and nods, pursing her plump rose petal lips so they drain of blood.

I wonder how it must be for her, having so much history with so many of the council members. Zeus gave me my position out of necessity, for a favour he needed me to do, and Aphrodite's place beside me was my stipulation. She had not wanted to work with Ares, nor with his father, and yet she does so with a courage I could not muster.

Her silence speaks volumes, and where a mortal woman in one of the many love stories inspired by the muses under my command might immediately complain, her longevity and subtle beauty inclines her to a graceful wordlessness instead.

I take a spritely step forward, the thud of my rubber boot dulled by the blue velvet of the carpet beneath our feet. We travel beneath the length of the awning's metallic sheen, approaching a bulky tanned doorman in a matching toga to the valet, who pulls open the glass door. I bid Aphrodite enter first, following behind her fluidly and leaving the crowd of bystanders hungry for whatever it is they desire of us.

Within, I relax a little more. The familiar domed ceiling traps wild lightning bolts that crackle in every direction and at every angle, forking through the air and providing a blatant strobe effect throughout the bar.

Aphrodite shrugs the diamond encrusted shawl from her shoulders, inhaling deeply.

I wonder what she's smelling, what the ambrosia's aromatic tease is conjuring for her with its knowing magic that flies between the synapses of the mind while unlocking the soul. For me, it's simple. Cherry blossoms on a fresh morning breeze, the pure glacial water of a mountain spring mixing with the clay of a modest riverbank.

The ambrosia takes you on a journey, on a sensory experience that allows you to follow the path of its energetic components from the barrenness of the farrow fields to the rich succulence of the flowering fruit itself.

It's the perfect way to get out of our own heads, to help us reflect, and remind us we are all a part of something much larger, that even Immortals are but energy that will move through time and space in one form or another, never resting or staying still, eternal but ever changing and infallible.

Even as gods, we might keep ourselves intact, be permanent and never return to the Crucible from which we once came, but we will not be flesh puppeteers forever.

I could be the soil beneath your feet next Tuesday, a cresting wave tomorrow afternoon.

Aphrodite lets the diamond encrusted silk hang limp from her hand, though the surface of the material comes alive from the light which slashes across the space without apology or restraint. Scolding myself to focus on the night ahead, and not the crystal's fractal splendour, I take her hand once more.

We wander, with patrons' eyes turning to us as expected, from the entranceway and over to the circular marble bar that lines up exactly with the dome of the ceiling overhead.

The centre of the bar does not hold just any liquor, but the golden honey I would accept from no other venue but one owned by Hermes. A shrewd businessman, anyone who's anyone knows he is the purveyor of the finest quality products in Olympus, and Aphrodite, if not I, deserves the best.

A bartender in a uniform toga, his garment held tight over his torso by a ruby broach this time, inquires about what I'm in the mood for, but tonight isn't about me. He has dull silver eyes and a smattering of dark chest hair that vibrates with his breast as his pecs rise and fall, and his head boasts a full mop of dark strands, unextraordinary in every regard.

"I'll have whatever the lady is having." I glimpse at Aphrodite, who lays the pad of her index finger against the curve of her bottom lip, eyes scanning the glass Ambrosia fountain beyond. The eyes of the Titan bartender watch her, enraptured, as she orders. He doesn't answer, so I cough loudly, breaking his evident trance.

"I said, I'll take something from the fall of late last year, something warm and bright. Not too close to the winter, though—" she repeats herself, and he nods as I stare blankly at him, unamused. She doesn't need random bartenders ogling her right now, even if she is *the* Aphrodite.

"Feeling empty?" I whisper, and she frowns.

"Is it so obvious?" she mumbles under her breath, nervously brushing a strand of loose hair from the side of her face.

"Why do you think I brought you here?" I ask her, and she sighs out, breasts plumping themselves within the confines of her tight gown.

"I know, I just—" she begins her confessional, but I bring a finger to her lips.

"Wait, I had Hermes reserve us a private booth. You don't want your business all over town. You know how people gossip, especially about us," I remind her, and she nods, glancing over her shoulder. People are watching us, and I don't need to turn to know it. I can feel their eyes like diamond tipped drills pressing into the back of my neck, their judgemental intent sharp as the stone itself.

I pretend I'm oblivious, trying to focus on the bartender as he draws various measures of ambrosia, in hues ranging from mahogany syrup to palest honey, from glass taps that curve, their narrowness like the stems of flowers.

He fills two glasses until the contents of both shimmer a warm autumnal amber, setting down the fine stemmed vessels and sprinkling edible gold leaf atop the thick fizzing brew with a flourish of one practiced hand.

The scent of a crisp autumn breeze wafts up, curling and dancing as it first fills my nostrils and then my head. I take one glass as Aphrodite reaches for the other, letting my hand drop to the small of her back and ushering her toward a curved staircase.

She follows my lead, the puddle train of her sparkling rose gold gown following her as though it were liquid rather than silk. I watch as she ascends the cobalt runner, moving ahead of me, fingers tracing the curve of the balustrade with a provocative caress that she's probably unaware of. The eyes of the venue are upon her as she rises to the upper level, and I find the flush in their faces horribly predictable. I know, however, that if they could see beyond her face, they would be even more enraptured than they already are. A shame their interest is ever only skin deep.

She shimmies, hips swaying a circle eight as her buttocks rise and fall with each step she takes around the curved balcony that lines the far wall of the cylindrical room, finding our regular booth waiting for us.

She moves to take a seat, elegance unwavering as she parts the gossamer drapes that obscure us from the view of onlookers. I follow her, turning my back on the bar as I scoot across the golden upholstery, closing the drapes behind me. I find Hermes has placed fresh lightbloom in a simple glass vase in the centre of the circular white marble table, a gesture as thanks for our returning custom. The flowers light up Aphrodite's face from beneath, only causing her to radiate beauty even more.

She leans into me as I place an arm around her shoulder, inhaling the scent of her as though it were the scent of home and one so familiar that it is engrained into me on a level bone deep.

"So, tell me my dearest Aphrodite, what is it that troubles you so?" I demand, taking the first sip of my Ambrosia between expectant lips.

The beverage is the sensory story of an Indian summer that's overstayed its welcome into early September and is wrestling with the first rebellious turning leaves of an obstinate fall. It evokes the sound of crisp leaves crunching beneath nimble tread and the sudden chill that stings your nostrils and makes the blood rush uninhibited to your cheeks.

I swallow and take in the auburns, tangerines, and golden browns of thick dying canopies as they capture the low hanging sunlight of dusk, tainting my vision warm.

I smile up into Aphrodite's face.

"I just, you know—" The liquid mercury of her irises scorches the table with the pain of her gaze as she takes a diversionary sip of her own Ambrosia. I watch her intently, noting her lips exhaling a small whimper of appreciation as the cinnamon spiced autumnal twilight slides down the back of her throat in a hot torrent.

"No, I don't. That's why I brought you out tonight. You've been off all afternoon," I remind her, leaning back and appraising her face as her lips purse.

"I'm lonely, Apollo," she whispers, eyes dropping from mine as she moves to pluck a silken quicksilver petal from the light bloom in front of her. At the detachment of the petal, the entire thing flickers out, lighting her face no more.

"I'm not going to get offended; I'm going to wait for you to explain. Seeing as how I'm sitting right here and am devastatingly fun to be around." I let my lips curve up on the left side, flicking my head back so a scarlet lock of my hair is flung from my eyes.

"I mean romantically, you dick." She smacks me on the chest with the back of her heartbreakingly feminine hand, rolling those eyes as a reluctant smile creeps over her face.

"Aphrodite, goddess of love, made from the stuff, in fact, is romantically lonely?" I sound shocked, but it's for her benefit entirely. I've known she's lacking in that department for longer than I'd like to admit, perhaps selfishly, because I love having her as my roommate.

"Don't give me that. I know you know. You live right next door, for Hera's sake—" She takes another sip from her glass, eyelids fluttering with delayed pleasure as she crosses her legs, thigh rising between the slit in her skirt and forcing it wide.

"Oh, is that who you've been rubbing one out to every night? I had gathered it wasn't me." I cock an eyebrow, teasing her, and she almost spits out her drink.

"As the mortals would say, fuck off." She shakes her head, superior for a moment, before exhaling and slumping.

"If any of them hear you speak like that, I'm entirely sure you'll be single forever. Potty mouth isn't attractive," I remind her and she snorts.

"Since when did you have any authority on what's attractive? You're more likely to get a hard on for your paintbrush than an actual walking, talking soul," she reminds me, and I shrug. She's not wrong.

"So what? You're complaining because you're lonely — and yet, I'm fielding fifteen unexpected vagrants knocking on our front door of a regular Saturday night. You've seen your temple; it's not exactly like they don't have to employ a fleet of Titans to clear all the gifts men are leaving for you. I'm sure there's more than a few women among them too, if that's what you're into—" I query her, remembering her gaze scrutinising Hecate and Nemesis earlier today.

"You don't get it, do you? That's not love, that's just — *adoration.* Those people don't love me. They want to possess me like some kind of object. I've been through enough of that for a lifetime!" she huffs, cheeks flushing with hot, angry blood.

"Ahh, and so you refer to our favourite meathead, Ares, at last." I take a sip of my drink, remembering seeing her and the son of Zeus parading around town long before we were ever friends.

She and I were both young then, both foolish — although one might argue, given the conversation, that very little has changed.

"Ugh, don't even. You know he was just in it for the sex. We fought more than anything else. Total war monger, he just has to be right all the time." She's angry, the thought of him alone bringing malice to her tone. It suits her, and I smile, swallowing my drink and surveying her the entire time as her relationship history flickers through my head like an animator's sketchbook splayed open and ruffled by a sudden wild breeze.

"You don't say—" I joke, and she shrugs.

"I was a trophy to him more than anything, and you know what happens to trophies that lie in the hands of someone who isn't Zeus. Especially when that someone is his son. He can't bear not possessing the very best, the most coveted of all things."

I pale at the memory, where our friendship had first taken root, blossomed amid her life's fiercest emotional storm. I had found her, crying, in a secluded corner of the Othrysian Orchard where she'd been raped by Zeus after arguing with Ares about his lack of interest in anything other than her body.

It seems, I had thought as I kicked one of the apples that lay scattered and smashed around her, gown ripped asunder, *that the apple has not fallen far from the tree.*

She had sworn never to tell another soul, for it would only hurt Ares. Foolishly, with a tender heart and broken soul, Aphrodite had never dared, and not even her ex-husband knew in the short time they were married.

"And what about Hephaestus?" I prompt her, curious, remembering how much of a phenomenon the wedding had been.

"What about him? You know we got divorced for a reason." She sounds bored, running the tip of her finger around the rim of her glass. Olympolis, in its entirety, was abuzz about that wedding for months, but only I had known the truth as she vetoed divine gown after divine gown. I watched her spin and pout, but I knew it wasn't the dress at all causing her restlessness and indecision; it was the groom.

She had married Heph as protection. Protection from future heartbreak, from her honour being torn to tatters any further.

For who would try to undermine the master forger who provides the weapons for the gods themselves?

Aphrodite had been smart, knowing that Zeus nor Ares would dare spite themselves by getting on Hephaestus' bad side, but it had come, as these things always do, at a cost.

She didn't love him; they were friends, but that was all. He would spend most of his time up in the belly of Vulcan while she spent his considerable fortune on the most beautiful objects Olympus had to offer.

I mean, there's a reason she has the biggest room in the entire house to herself. Most of it is for her wardrobe alone, and I've had to have an ensuite built on to her bedchamber as well, because sharing a bathroom may well have meant the end of our friendship. After all, I might be a god and everything, but even gods need to pee at least once a day.

Still, even though she has a closet bursting at its glimmering seams and enough beauty products to sink the Occulta Mirum to even greater depths, she found she couldn't buy happiness. The nights we spent in ambrosia bars, her fear and indecision about ending things in order to pursue her heart, had been excruciating.

That's why when I took the position on the Aetherial Court, her seat next to mine had been my one and only condition. Her being on the council gave her a new kind of protection and the freedom to end her marriage behind closed doors. Zeus is watched closely by the other council members, especially Ares and Hera, closely enough that he would never dare touch Aphrodite in meetings or the Council Chambers with so many other powerful eyes watching.

I look into her face, as her own eyes glaze over with memories, and think back on today.

"I get the impression this isn't something you've been dwelling on for a while. This is something that's recent. So — what's happened today?" I tilt my head, rainbow brows pinching together in the centre of my flawlessly porcelain forehead.

She bites her bottom lip.

"Aphrodite—" I begin, but then my eyes widen. The council chambers were the same today as they ever were before, except—

"Haedes." The word is enough, and her entire face flushes pink, eyes tinging the colour of rose-tinted glasses. She stutters to reply, but I interrupt her, leaning forward with a gasp. "Oh my God. It *is* Haedes!" I exclaim, heart stopping a second beneath my breast.

When the hell did that happen? How did I not notice?

"Shhh, keep your voice down!" She smacks me on the bicep again, this time intending to leave a resounding sting. "And wipe that look of damn shock off your face before I slap it off," she spits, eyes narrowing and cheeks pinching as her nostrils flare.

I sit back, thinking for a moment, trying to recall an instance when their attraction has been obvious to me. A single moment when the idea of a relationship between them had seemed tangible instead of a teenage poet's wet dream.

Ideas whip themselves into an excited tornado between my ears, melancholy symphonies screaming above the wind.

A taboo connection between death and love.

How deliciously rich in artistic promise.

My silence evidently riles her, my eyes snapping back to her face as she hisses. "Please, stop looking at me like that. It's like you're watching Ares rescue a kitten from a tree—"

"Sorry, I just — this is so unexpected. I never thought — I didn't even know you knew one another outside of political circles." I try not to sound as surprised as I really am, but I watch the flush in her cheeks die a little as her gaze becomes steel.

"Well, I do have *some* secrets. Haedes and I, well, we were friends when I was a very young girl. Before his banishment. He hated his home life, and my parents weren't around, so we kind of gravitated towards one another," she explains, a rosewater mist clouding her gaze as memories flood across the desert of her mind.

"And you still have feelings? After all this time?" I lean forward, cupping my hand in my palm, a dreaminess overtaking my face.

"Apollo, please. Try not to make too much of this. Nothing will ever come of it, and besides, I'm not even sure if we *had* anything. He just — he *saw* me. Not just my face but who I am." Her voice becomes strained and pained as her forehead gives the slightest sign that it might crease, but then it relaxes without a fight into the flawless silk I'm so used to admiring.

"What do you mean, nothing will ever come of it? But—" I think of all the reasons things *should* come of it. I don't like Haedes that much, it's known, but that's mainly because I don't know him, and everything I do know has Zeus at its source and is possibly biased. He's never been around that much, and to be honest, everybody just thinks he's kind of strange.

"Apollo, stop. Please. I love you. You know that, and I know you want me to be happy. Haedes and I—" Her irises tinge pink yet again. "It can never be, and that's the end of it."

"I don't suppose you're going to give me a reason *why* this is so doomed?" I reply with haughty impatience, irritated at her for the first time tonight. She's being overdramatic, and that's my forte.

"Look, firstly, he's Zeus' brother. Can you imagine?" She has a point, and the silence between us becomes heavy like a wet blanket. My face is sullen.

"And secondly?" I demand, watching her shift uncomfortably.

"Secondly, his reputation isn't exactly the kind I want to be attached to. He fell in love with a mortal, you know!" She says this like it's a crime.

"And?" I press her, trying to get her to spill the real reason she's so reluctant to give the idea of this a chance.

"And, *she's dead.* Gone. Soul incinerated. How can I possibly compete with that?" I snort, and she rolls her eyes before continuing, "Besides, he's weird, Apollo. Nemesis had him and Thanatos around for dinner the other night, and apparently, he spent the entire meal trying to explain some insane human custom to do with destroying hardboiled balls of sugar. We just — we aren't kids anymore. We have grown apart and belong in two separate worlds." She takes a slug of the golden brew that fizzes on within her glass, wincing at the sudden sensory onslaught.

I sigh, exasperated in more ways than one.

"You're afraid." I assess her, drumming my fingers in a distracting rhythm on my knee, trying to sort out my thoughts on it all.

"Love and death cannot survive one another. It's just not possible," she says this, definite.

"And yet, you are concerned he pines for the deceased and departed. Worried that the fragility of a mortal makes her more precious and more valuable than you. Funny, isn't it?" I quip, and her face turns stony.

"Shut up."

The conversation dies right there between us as I reluctantly change the subject. I have discovered what ails her, but I also know that if it is true, the feelings between Aphrodite and Haedes will blossom in their own time. The artist of courtship between them is still clearly stuck for inspiration.

For her sake, I want to see them come together, want to see her taken care of and happy. See her protected from those who would do her harm and at the same time see her romantically fulfilled.

And yet...

ALSO BY

QUEENS OF FANTASY SHORTS AND NOVELLAS

OTHER GENRES FROM KRISTY NICOLLE

DYSTOPIAN ROMANCE:

Something Blue- A Dystopian Romance Standalone

POETRY:

I Am Arcana- A Tarot Inspired Poetry Collection

Starsong- A Zodiac Inspired Poetry Collection

To keep up to date with the latest release dates, spin offs, and exclusive content, head on over to kristynicolle.com

ABOUT THE AUTHOR

30-Year-Old British Author of Award-Winning Indie Fantasy Romance, Kristy Nicolle is escaping the pain of Ehlers Danlos Syndrome by crafting intricate and immersive worlds for her readers. She lives in Norwich, Norfolk, with her long-time life partner Mark, and can often be found writing in her local coffee shop - *Botany and Beans,* with a peppermint mocha, surrounded by beloved witchy paraphernalia and plants she knows only too well she'd kill at home.

FOLLOW KRISTY ON SOCIAL MEDIA OR FIND HER AT KRISTYNICOLLE.COM